OAK PARK PUBLIC LIBRARY

3 1132 00837 9525

JAN - - 2004

W9-COF-488

To Fred and Dragica

Copyright © 2003 by Marie-Louise Gay

All rights reserved. No part of this publication may be reproduced, stored in a retrieval system or transmitted, in any form or by any means, without the prior written consent of the publisher or a licence from The Canadian Copyright Licensing Agency (Access Copyright). For an Access Copyright licence, visit www.accesscopyright.ca or call toll free to 1-800-893-5777

Groundwood Books / Douglas & McIntyre
720 Bathurst Street, Suite 500, Toronto, Ontario
Distributed in the USA by Publishers Group West
1700 Fourth Street, Berkeley, CA 94710

We acknowledge for their financial support of our publishing program the Canada Council for the Arts, the Ontario Arts Council and the Government of Canada through the Book Publishing Industry Development Program (BPIDP).

ONTARIO ARTS COUNCIL
CONSEIL DES ARTS DE L'ONTARIO

National Library of Canada Cataloging in Publication
Gay, Marie-Louise
Good night Sam / Marie-Louise Gay
ISBN 0-88899-530-X
I. Title
PS8563.A868G663 2003   C813'.54   C2003-900197-0
PZ7

Library of Congress Control Number: 2002117358

Printed and bound in China

OAK PARK PUBLIC LIBRARY
ADELE H. MAZE BRANCH

GOOD NIGHT
SAM

MARIE-LOUISE GAY

A GROUNDWOOD BOOK DOUGLAS & McINTYRE TORONTO VANCOUVER BERKELEY

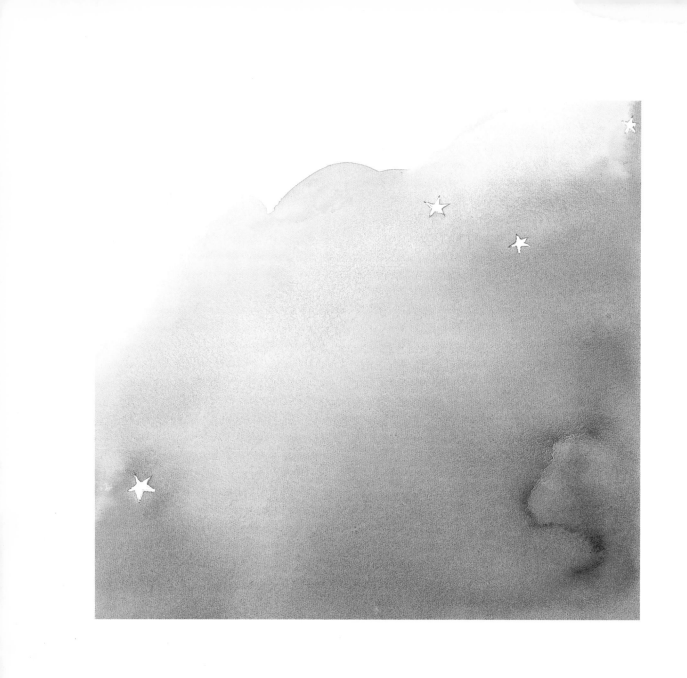

"Stella," whispered Sam, "are you sleeping?"
"Yes," answered Stella. "Aren't you?"

"No, said Sam. "I can't sleep."
"Why? Are you having a bad dream?"

"No," answered Sam. "I can't sleep without Fred."

"Where is he?" asked Stella.
"I don't know."

"Did you look under your bed?"
"He's not there," said Sam.
"Fred sneezes when he's under the bed."

"Maybe he's outside," said Stella.

"It's too dark outside," said Sam.
"Fred is afraid of the dark."

"Look in the closet," said Stella.
"A monster lives in that closet," said Sam.
"Fred would never go in there."

"Go to sleep, Sam," yawned Stella.
"I can't sleep without Fred," said Sam.

"Why don't you try counting sheep?" asked Stella.
"Sheep? What sheep?"

"First you close your eyes," said Stella.
"And imagine hundreds of sheep. Then you count them."
"I can only count to three," said Sam.

"I guess we'll have to look for Fred," sighed Stella.
"I know he isn't downstairs," said Sam.
"Fred doesn't like those strange noises."

"That's only the clock ticking, Sam. Come on."

"Maybe he's in the living-room," said Stella.
"Behind the couch or under the big armchair."

"Fred never goes near that chair," said Sam.
"He thinks it looks like a giant toad."

"Look!" cried Sam. "A ghost!"

"That's the moon, Sam."

"If Fred was here," said Sam, "he would bark at the moon."

"Fred never barks," said Stella.
"Yes, he does," whispered Sam.
"Fred barks when he's afraid."

"I'm tired, Sam. We'll look for Fred tomorrow."
"Will we get up early?" asked Sam.

"We'll get up with the birds," answered Stella.
"Birds? What birds?"
"Come on, Sam," sighed Stella.

"Stella!" cried Sam. "I found Fred!"
"Where?"

"He was sleeping under my quilt," said Sam.
"Good!" yawned Stella. "Let's sleep too."

"Stella?" whispered Sam. "I still can't sleep."
"Why not?"
"Fred is snoring too loudly," said Sam.

"Good night, Sam," sighed Stella.